Jack

and the
Beanstalk

In memory of Richard Walker

For my Grandparents
May and Grania
and in memory of
Richard and Joe — *N. S.*

Barefoot Books
37 West 17th Street
4th Floor East
New York, New York
10011

Text copyright © 1999 by Richard Walker
Illustrations copyright © 1999 by Niamh Sharkey

Illustrations prepared in oil and gesso on canvas
Typeset in Monotype Bembo Bold 20pt on 32pt leading

Graphic design by Design/Section, Frome
Color reproduction by Grafiscan, Verona
Printed and bound in Singapore by Tien Wah Press (Pte) Ltd

1 3 5 7 9 8 6 4 2

Publisher Cataloging-in-Publication Data

Walker, Richard.
  Jack and the beanstalk / retold by Richard Walker ; illustrated by
Niamh Sharkey.—1st ed.
[40]p. : col. ill. ;   cm.
Summary: Classic fairy tale, retold with sparky originality and lively
humor, complemented by fascinatingly offbeat illustrations.
ISBN 1-902283-13-9
1. Fairy tales. 2. Folklore — England. 3. Giants — Folklore. I. Sharkey,
Niamh, ill. II. Title.
398.2/ 094 2/ 02 [E]—dc21 1999   AC   CIP

Jack
and the
Beanstalk

retold by
Richard Walker

Illustrated by
Niamh Sharkey

BAREFOOT BOOKS

I'm not going to start by saying that Jack was lazy. When there was an adventure in the offing, he was not lazy at all. But most of the time, he just did a little bit of this and a little bit of that.

Jack lived with his mom and Daisy, the cow, in a tumbledown farmhouse, a little way out of town. Jack's mom liked to do just a little bit of this and a little bit of that as well. They didn't have very much money, but they didn't much care.

Then one day
there was nothing
left to eat, not even
a crust of old bread,
and no money left
either to buy anything.

"It's no good, Jack," his mom said. "We'll have
to sell poor old Daisy. You had better get up
early tomorrow morning and take her to market.
Make sure you get a good price for her!"

Jack knew better than to argue. Besides, he was very hungry. So the next day he got up at sunrise and set off down the lane with Daisy in tow.

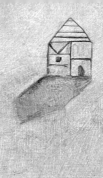

He had not gone far when he came
around a corner and bumped into a funny
little man. The man was wearing a big,
baggy jacket with big, baggy pockets.

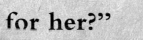

"Good morning to you!" said the man.
"That's a nice-looking cow
you have there. Do you
fancy doing a swap
for her?"

Jack remembered what his mom had told him, so he asked, "What will you give me in exchange?"

"These!" declared the funny little man and, plunging a hand deep into one of his pockets, he pulled out six plump beans.

"Those?" asked Jack.

"Yes," said the funny little man, "these! Don't think these are just ordinary beans. Oh no! These are magic beans. But you will have to be careful with them. I've lost the instructions for them, so I'm not sure what they do."

Well, there was nothing Jack loved better than magic, so he handed over Daisy, took the beans and hurried home.

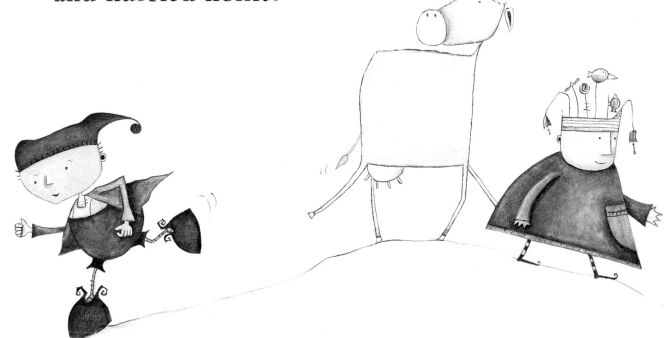

As soon as he reached the back door, Jack burst into the kitchen and proudly threw the beans down on the table.

"What's this?" exclaimed his mom.

"Oh dear," thought Jack.

"They're magic beans, Mom. I swapped
them for Daisy. At least we've got something
to eat...well, we will have when they've grown."
Jack's mom was furious. She went white
in the face and shouted and stamped.
Then she threw open the window
and flung the beans outside.
That night, Jack and his
mom went to bed
feeling miserable
and hungry.

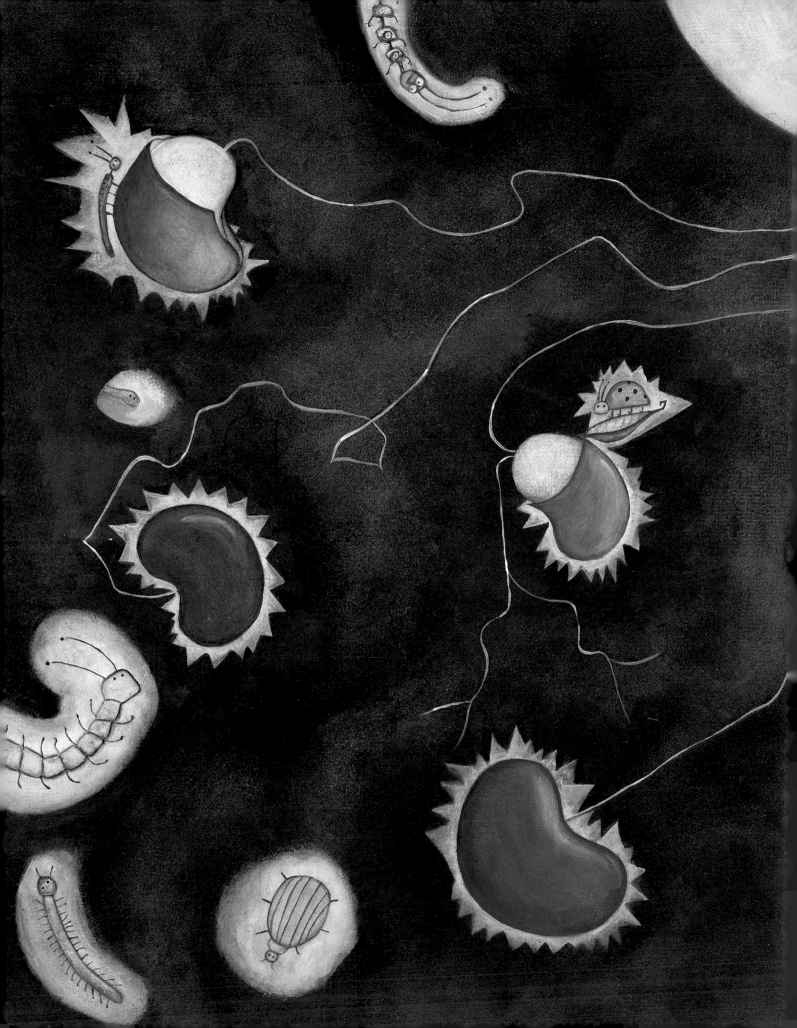

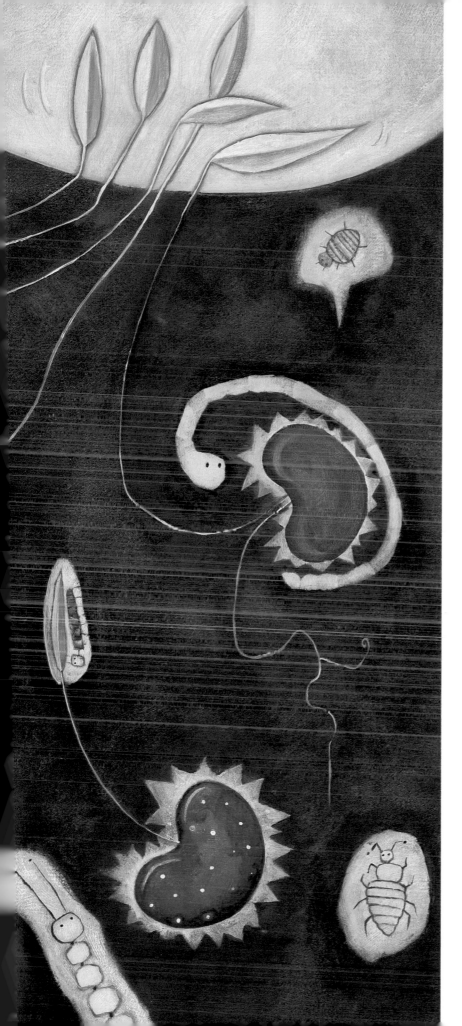

But in the garden, things began to happen. The beans slipped down through cracks in the ground. Their roots wriggled deep into the earth and shoots pushed upward. They burst through the hard crust of the soil and, twisting and tangling together, they grew high into the sky. They kept on growing and growing until they reached the land of the clouds.

Then a long, wiry tendril reached down to the house and tapped on Jack's bedroom window.

"Who's that?" Jack yawned. He saw strange shadows in the moonlit window and, not sure whether this was a dream or a real adventure, he padded across the room and drew back his curtains. There, bending and swaying in the moonlight, was the most enormous beanstalk he had ever seen.

"I wonder where the top of it goes to?" Jack said to himself.

There was only one way to find out. Without stopping to think twice, he clambered over the windowsill and started to climb. Soon the house was just a tiny dot, far below. Still he made his way upward.

Finally he reached the land of the clouds and stepped off the beanstalk onto the fluffy gray ground. In the distance, he could see a huge castle. Jack walked straight up to it and knocked on the door. He heard the clank of keys being

turned, the rumble of bars being slid back and
the rattle of chains being unfastened. Then, at
last, the huge door creaked open a crack and he
saw a little old woman peering at him by the
light of a candle.

"You can't come in!" she whispered. "He'll be back soon.

GO AWAY!"

"Please!" Jack begged. "I'm a stranger here and starving hungry. Can't I just pop in quickly for something to eat?"

The woman looked at him more closely and saw that he was a nice-looking lad with a ready smile.

"Very well, you can come in for a minute," she said, "but don't let him catch sight of you."

"Who's *he*?" asked Jack as they made their way along the dusty castle corridors to the big kitchen. Lining the walls were mounds of huge, bulging sacks, which jingled as Jack brushed against them.

"The giant, of course. If he catches you, he'll eat you for sure. He's got a foul temper so you'd better

keep out of his way. Hide among the sacks if you hear him coming."

Then, just as she finished speaking, there was a crashing of heavy footsteps outside the room. Jack only just managed to hide behind a heap of sacks when the door burst open and in barged the giant.

"FEE, FI, FO, FUM!

...I smell the blood of a stinky man! Where is he, woman? Where are you hiding him?" The giant sniffled his way around the room until he came close to where Jack was hiding.

"Oh, don't be silly!" said the old woman. "All you can smell is the stew I've made. I was trying a bowl of it to make sure it was good enough for you. Would you like some?"

Soon the giant had slurped his way through an enormous bowl of stew. He belched loudly, then demanded, "Fetch me my goose! I want some more gold!"

The old woman slipped out of the room and was soon back, cradling a huge, very gloomy-looking bird in her arms. Peeping out from his hiding place, Jack watched as the goose began to lay eggs — each one made of pure gold. As each egg appeared, the giant put it into a giant egg box. Then he demanded, "Now fetch me my harp. I want some music!"

Once again, the old woman bustled out of the room and came back holding an exquisite

 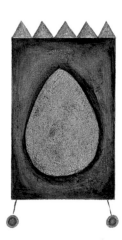  

harp made of pure gold. Even the strings were golden. "Play, harp, play!" shouted the giant... And, as if by magic, the room was filled with

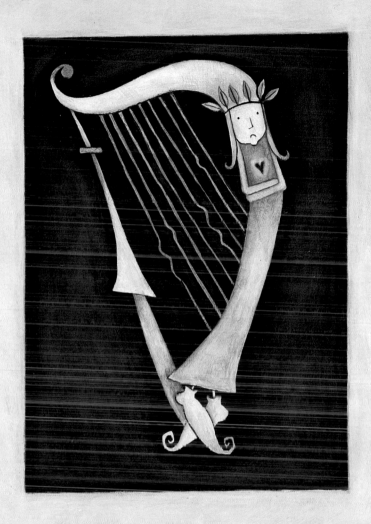

the most beautiful, gentle music as the strings began to vibrate all by themselves. Soon the giant fell asleep and his snuffling and snoring echoed around the room.

Jack crept out from his hiding place and quietly began to drag one of the bulging sacks, full of gold coins, across the kitchen floor. It was very heavy and it jingled as he pulled it, but the giant did not stir. Jack heaved and heaved and dragged the sack right out of the castle, across the cloud and back to the top of the beanstalk. The sack was too heavy for him to carry any further so he left it there and slid quickly down.

When he reached
home, Jack found
his mom staring up
at the beanstalk and
scratching her head.
"Rope!" cried Jack
as he sprang to the
ground. He ran off
to the shed and
came back a few
moments later with
great coils wrapped
around him. Then
he set off back up
the beanstalk.

After a while, he felt the rope become loose, and he knew that the sack had reached the ground safely and that his mom had untied it.

At the top of the beanstalk, Jack tied one end of the rope to the stem and the other to the sack of gold. Then he started to lower the sack.

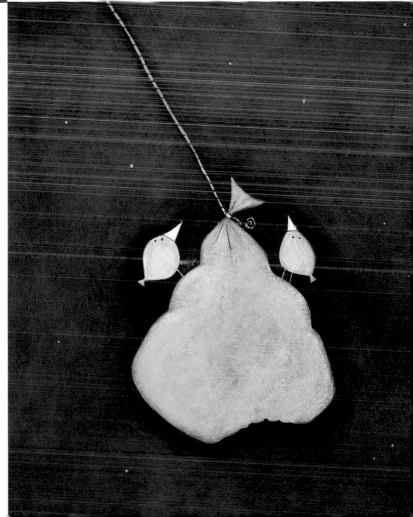

Jack headed back to the kitchen to fetch another sack. As he crept past the giant, the goose looked up hopefully and whispered, "Can I come too? I hate it up here. You wouldn't need to take the sack then. I could lay you as many golden eggs as you want."

So Jack picked her up and ran out of the room. In the corridor, he bumped into the old woman.

"Can I come with you as well?" she asked.
"Of course," said Jack. "Here, you take the
goose and I'll go back for the harp."

But as Jack picked up the harp,
it suddenly cried out, "What's going on?
Who are you? Help! Help!" Jack raced
out of the kitchen just as the giant woke up,
saw what was happening and began to give chase.
Faster and faster ran Jack. Closer and closer came
the giant.

As he reached the top of the beanstalk, Jack could
feel the giant's hand on his neck.

'Quick!' he shouted.

The old woman started slithering down with the goose. Jack slithered down behind her with the harp. They could hear the giant shouting and swearing as he tried to follow them.

The beanstalk bent and swayed
wildly, first to the left and then to
the right, but the old woman and
Jack reached the ground safely.

Jack grabbed the rope.
He pulled and he pulled
until he could see the
giant, hanging on for
dear life, glaring
down at him.
Then he let go.

The beanstalk shot upright
like an enormous catapult. Unable
to hold on any longer, the giant flew
off the end. He soared away into space
and was never seen again. And, as
far as I know, he's still there.

The old woman went inside to make a pot of tea. Mom put the golden harp on the kitchen dresser, and Jack made the magic goose a special hut. He put the sack of gold in the cellar and took out a coin whenever he needed to buy something. And the last time I went to visit, the harp played jigs and reels, so we all had a merry dance.

BAREFOOT BOOKS publishes high-quality picture books for children of all ages and specializes in the work of artists and writers from many cultures. If you have enjoyed this book and would like to receive a copy of our current catalog, please contact our New York office —
Barefoot Books, 37 West 17th Street, 4th Floor East, New York, New York, 10011
e-mail: ussales@barefoot-books.com
website: www.barefoot-books.com